DRAGON MASTERS

RISE OF THE EARTH DRAGON

BY

TRACEY WEST

ILLUSTRATED BY

GRAHAM HOWELLS

SCHOLASTIC INC.

DRAGON MASTERS
Read All the Books
1
DRAGON MASTERS
RISE OF THE EARTH DRAGON
TRACEY WEST
SCHOLASTIC
2
DRAGON MASTERS
SAVING THE SUN DRAGON
TRACEY WEST
SCHOLASTIC
3
DRAGON MASTERS
SECRET OF THE WATER DRAGON
TRACEY WEST
SCHOLASTIC
4
DRAGON MASTERS
POWER OF THE FIRE DRAGON
TRACEY WEST
SCHOLASTIC

TABLE OF CONTENTS

FOR LAUREN,

the girl who loved dragons—and still does.

—TW

Library of Congress Cataloging-in-Publication Data
West, Tracey, 1965- author.
Rise of the earth dragon / by Tracey West.
pages cm. — (Dragon masters ; 1)
Eight-year-old Drake is snatched up by the King's soldiers and taken to the castle where he is told by the wizard Griffith that he has been chosen to be a Dragon Master like Ana, Rori, and Bo — and his first task will be to discover whether his dragon, Worm, has any special powers.
ISBN 0-545-64623-5 (pbk. : alk. paper) — ISBN 0-545-64624-3 (hardcover : alk. paper) — ISBN 0-545-64633-2 (ebook)
1. Dragons — Juvenile fiction. 2. Wizards — Juvenile fiction. 3. Magic — Juvenile fiction. [1. Dragons — Fiction. 2. Wizards — Fiction. 3. Magic — Fiction.] I. Title.
PZ7.W51937Ri 2014
[Fic] — dc23
2013046258

ISBN 978-0-545-64624-6 (hardcover) / ISBN 978-0-545-64623-9 (paperback)

10 9 8 7 6 5 4 3 2 14 15 16 17 18 19/0

Printed in China 38
First Scholastic printing, September 2014
Illustrated by Graham Howells
Edited by Katie Carella
Book design by Jessica Meltzer

CHAPTER 1

TO THE CASTLE!

Drake didn't see the king's soldier coming. He was busy digging in the onion patch. He pulled out a fat, white onion. A worm crawled on it. Drake didn't mind the worm. He was the son of a farmer. His family had been growing onions in the Kingdom of Bracken forever. He would spend his life digging up onions, whether he wanted to or not.

Drake picked up the worm.

"Hello, little guy," he said. Then he put the worm back in the dirt.

"Are you Drake?" a loud voice asked behind him.

Drake jumped and turned around. One of the king's soldiers rode up on a black horse. He had a yellow beard. His shirt had a gold dragon sewn on it — the symbol of King Roland the Bold.

"Yes, I'm Drake," Drake said, his voice shaking. Soldiers never came to the fields. Not unless a farmer was in trouble.

The soldier rode up to Drake. He reached down and pulled him up onto his horse.

"Hey, what are you doing?" Drake yelled. The soldier didn't answer.

Drake's mother ran out of their hut.

"Wait! Where are you taking my boy?" she yelled.

"To King Roland," the soldier said.

Drake's heart jumped a little. He had always wanted to meet the king.

"But he's only eight!" his mother yelled. She marched up to the horse.

"The king has chosen him," the soldier said.

Chosen me for what? Drake wondered. He knew better than to ask the soldier questions. Peasants like Drake weren't allowed to speak unless spoken to.

"The king will take good care of him," the soldier said. Then he spurred on the horse, and sped off.

"Drake, do as the king says!" his mother called out.

Drake had never been on a horse before. He held on tight.

Drake's heart pumped fast as they raced through the village. They raced over the stone bridge. Finally, they stopped in front of King Roland's castle.

The soldier helped Drake climb down from the horse. He opened the castle door and gave Drake a shove. They passed paintings and statues and people in fancy clothes. The soldier stomped behind Drake as they walked through the halls. Drake wanted to look at everything, but the soldier gave him a push whenever he slowed down.

Then they came to some stairs. They walked down . . . down . . . down. The soldier stopped at a door.

"Where are we going?" Drake finally asked.

"*We* are not going anywhere," the soldier said. "Good luck." Then he ran back up the stairs.

"Hey! What do you mean?" Drake yelled. But he was all alone.

Drake looked at the big, stone door. He felt afraid. But more than that, he was curious. He pushed it open and saw . . .

. . . the face of a giant, red dragon!

Drake blinked. He didn't believe his eyes. Then—*whoosh!* — the dragon shot a huge fireball from his mouth!

THE DRAGON STONE

Drake dove away from the door. The fireball just missed him!

"Vulcan, stand down!" he heard someone yell.

Drake stood up. A red-haired girl was standing in the doorway.

"No more fireballs!" she yelled at the dragon. He had shiny red scales and a long, thick tail. Two big wings grew out of his back.

Dragons aren't real, thought Drake. But Drake could see the dragon. And he had felt the heat from the fireball.

A tall man walked past the girl. He had a long, white beard. He wore a pointy hat and a dark green robe.

"Welcome, Drake," the man said. "I am Griffith, the king's wizard."

Did he say "wizard"? Drake had so many questions! "Is that a dragon?" he asked.

"He's not just *a* dragon," said the girl. "He's *my* dragon. Vulcan is the *best* dragon in the kingdom."

"Drake, meet Rori," Griffith said. "Rori, please take Vulcan away. Tell the others I will be there shortly."

Others? Drake thought.

The girl sighed. "Fine. Let's go, Vulcan." She led the dragon away.

Then the wizard led Drake down a dark hall.

"Why am I here, sir?" Drake asked.

Griffith didn't answer. He stopped in front of a door. Griffith pointed at its big, brass lock. Sparks flew from his finger. The lock opened.

Drake's eyes grew wide. *Wizard magic!* he thought.

He followed Griffith into a room piled high with strange things. He saw bottles filled with colorful waters and powders.

Griffith picked up a wooden box. The box was carved with pictures of dragons.

"This is why you are here," he said, opening the box.

Drake peered inside. A green stone as big as his head glittered in the light.

"This Dragon Stone told me you have the heart of a dragon," said the wizard. He tapped Drake's chest.

"It d-did?" Drake asked. His eyes got big.

"Yes. And those with the heart of a dragon become Dragon Masters for King Roland," Griffith said.

Drake had heard stories about the magical Dragon Stone. But he had never believed they were real. Now all his questions came spilling out.

"How does the stone *know* I have the heart of a dragon? And how did you find me? And what's a Dragon Master? And why does King Roland want Dragon Masters?"

"The stone is old and mysterious," Griffith said. "Even I do not fully understand its magic. A Dragon Master is able to connect with dragons. As for the king . . . he is very fond of dragons. But he cannot control them."

"So Vulcan isn't the only dragon?" Drake asked.

The wizard grinned. "No, he is not."

He handed Drake a green stone on a gold chain. "This is a piece of the Dragon Stone," he said. "It will help you connect with your dragon."

Drake's heart jumped. *My dragon? I get a dragon?* he thought. He slipped the stone into his pocket.

"Be careful, Drake," the wizard warned. "Dragons are dangerous. And even the Dragon Stone can't protect you from their powers."

"What powers?" Drake asked.

The wizard led him away without another word.

CHAPTER 3

MORE DRAGONS!

Drake's mind was spinning as he left the wizard's workshop. He followed Griffith to a big underground room. There were no windows. Torches hung on the walls. Drake saw Rori and Vulcan. He also saw two more kids — and two more dragons!

"Drake, this is Bo," Griffith said, pointing to a boy with black hair, "and his dragon, Shu."

Bo was petting his dragon's tail. This dragon had shiny blue scales, but no wings.

"Hi," Drake said.

"Nice to meet you, Drake," the boy said politely.

Griffith led Drake over to a girl with long, black hair. Her dragon had white scales. A yellow band of scales circled the dragon's neck. The tips of its wings were yellow, too.

"This is Ana, and her dragon, Kepri," Griffith said.

Drake nodded. "Hi," he said.

"We could use somebody new around here," Ana said with a grin.

"You have met the other Dragon Masters and their dragons. It is time for you to meet *your* dragon," Griffith said.

Drake's heart pounded. *My family will never believe this!* he thought. *Just this morning I was digging onions. Now I have ridden a horse. I've met a wizard. I've seen the Dragon Stone. And I'm going to have my very own dragon?!*

He and the other Dragon Masters followed Griffith down another dark hallway.

"The dragons sleep in caves when they're not training," Bo explained as they walked.

"Vulcan's cave is the biggest," bragged Rori.

Griffith stopped in front of a small cave. Wood bars covered the cave.

"Drake, meet your dragon!" the wizard said.

CHAPTER 4

WORM

Drake peered inside the dark cave. A dragon sat inside. *Well, this creature kind of looks like a dragon*, Drake thought. The dragon had brown scales that weren't shiny. He had two tiny wings. He had big, green eyes, and little ears. And he didn't have legs! He looked like a big snake.

The only dragon-like thing about him seemed to be his long snout.

Drake stepped up to the wood bars. "Hi, dragon. I'm Drake."

The dragon didn't move.

"Put on the stone," Griffith said.

Drake slipped the green stone around his neck. He felt a tingly feeling all over his body.

Right away, the dragon lifted his head. He stared at Drake with his big, green eyes. Drake felt a strange chill.

Griffith stepped forward. "You must name your dragon," he said.

Rori piped up. "Good luck naming *him*. He looks boring."

"How about Noodle Head?" Ana asked with a giggle.

Bo shook his head. "No, this dragon needs a good name."

Drake looked carefully at the dragon. He looked at his long, brown body.

"Worm," he said. "His name is Worm."

"That is a good name for an Earth Dragon," said Griffith, opening the gate. "Now, Drake, ask Worm to follow you."

"Okay," Drake said. "Worm, please follow me."

Worm crawled forward.

"Good work!" said the wizard. "Keep it up, Drake."

"Come on," Drake said, starting to walk down the hallway. Worm crawled after him.

"He really is like a big, ugly worm," Rori said.

"Rori, be nice," said Ana.

Drake didn't say anything. Worm *was* like a big worm.

"Where are we going?" he asked.

"To the Training Room," Griffith replied.

"Yeah," said Rori. "We'll see what you and your dragon are made of."

Drake felt nervous. He touched his Dragon Stone. *How am I supposed to train a dragon?* he thought. *What if I fail? What if I'm not a Dragon Master after all?*

CHAPTER 5

DO SOMETHING!

The Training Room was one big, open space. Shields and long poles hung from the walls. Buckets held water and sand. And at one end of the room was a round target. Straw stuffing poked out from the sides.

Griffith pointed at the target. Sparks flew from his finger and a red bull's-eye showed up on the target.

"It's time for target practice!" the wizard said.

"Me first!" Rori called out. "Vulcan, come!"

The red dragon stomped forward.

"Vulcan, fire!" Rori yelled.

The dragon's orange eyes glowed. Then two streams of fire shot from his nose. The streams twisted together. The fire hit the bull's-eye.

"Perfect!" Rori cheered.

Then the straw burst into flames! Drake jumped back.

"Good aim," said Griffith. "Bo, can you help put the fire out?"

"Yes," said Bo. He looked at his dragon.

"Shu," he said simply. He didn't yell like Rori.

Shu swiftly crossed the room. *Did her feet even touch the ground?* wondered Drake.

"Water, please, Shu," Bo said.

A stream of water sprayed out of the blue dragon's mouth.

The fire sizzled. Water droplets danced in the air, lit up by the torches.

"Kepri! Rainbow time!" Ana cried.

Kepri glided across the room. Drake thought her white scales looked like jewels.

A soft beam of light came out of Kepri's mouth. It grew wider and wider. When it hit the water droplets, it made a rainbow!

"Wow," Drake said.

"Isn't she amazing?" asked Bo.

Ana smiled.

Rori put her hands on her hips.

"Now let's see what Worm can do," she said.

Drake felt nervous. He looked at Worm.

"Um, Worm, are you ready?" Drake asked.

Worm stared back at him.

I guess that means yes, thought Drake. "Okay, Worm. Fire!"

Drake jumped back in case fire came out of Worm's mouth. But Worm just lay there.

"Not all dragons can shoot fire," said Bo.

Drake nodded. "Right. Okay, Worm. Water!"

But Worm didn't shoot water.

"Ha!" Rori laughed. "I knew it. Worm can't do anything."

Drake's cheeks grew hot with anger. "He's just warming up," he said. "Come on, Worm. Shoot light out of your mouth!"

Still nothing.

"You call that a dragon?" Rori said.

"Please, Worm?" Drake whispered to his dragon. "Do something!"

Worm just blinked.

"Do not worry, Drake. Getting to know your dragon takes time," Griffith said. "Target practice is over for today. Let's go eat."

Bo grabbed Drake's elbow.

"I hope you're hungry, Drake! The Dragon Masters get as much food as we want," said Bo.

Drake was hungry so this news made him feel a little better. But he had failed the training. *How can I be a Dragon Master if my dragon won't do anything I ask it to do?* he thought. *I'm only an onion farmer. I don't belong here.*

CHAPTER 6

A NEW FRIEND

There was so much food on the dining room table! Roast chicken. Potatoes. Carrots. Bread. Cheese. It was more food than Drake had seen in his life.

"Pass the potatoes, please," Drake said.

Griffith pointed to the plate of potatoes. Sparks flew from his finger.

As the plate floated over to Drake, he forgot all about wanting to go home. He stabbed a potato with his fork.

"Is every supper like this?" Drake asked Bo.

Bo nodded. "Yes, there is always a great deal of good food," he said. "But sometimes I miss my mother's soup."

"Is your home kingdom far away?" Drake asked.

"Very far," said Bo. "I come from the east – the kingdom of Emperor Song."

"And I come from the south," added Ana. "It is warm there. Not cold and damp like it is here."

"Well, I am proud to be from *this* kingdom," Rori said. "My father is a blacksmith. He makes the best horseshoes in our village."

Drake missed home. He turned to Griffith.

"Is there a way I can let my family know I'm okay?" Drake asked.

The wizard nodded. "You may send them a note." He waved to one of the servants. "Please bring this boy paper and a quill."

A servant gave Drake paper, a small pot of ink, and a feather. Drake's cheeks turned red.

"What?" Rori asked. "Haven't you seen paper before?"

Drake looked down at his plate. "I worked in the fields at home," he said. "I never went to school. I know how to read. But we never had paper. Or quills. So I don't know how to write."

Rori started to say something, but Griffith gave her a hard look. Bo picked up the quill.

"I will write the note for you," he said.

"Thanks," Drake said. Then he told Bo what to write.

Dear Mother,

I am safe so please do not worry. Everything is new and exciting. The king is keeping me well fed. My new friend Bo helped me write this letter.

Love,

Drake

Drake did not say anything about dragons. He thought that might scare his mother.

The servant took the note away.

Drake yawned. "So, where do we sleep?"

"We have rooms in the tower," Bo said. "You will be in my room."

Drake smiled. "Good." At least he had one new friend here.

Suddenly, a soldier stomped into the room.

"All rise for King Roland the Bold!" he said.

CHAPTER 7

A STRANGE DREAM

The Dragon Masters jumped to their feet. King Roland swept into the room. He was a big man, with red hair and a bushy beard. He walked right up to Drake. Drake was so nervous, he was shaking.

"This is my new Dragon Master?" he asked.

"Yes, Your Highness," said Griffith.

The king frowned. "He's scrawny."

Drake felt like sinking into the floor.

The king turned to Griffith. "Explain this to me, wizard. My strongest men cannot control dragons. Why is it that these children can?"

"It is the way of the Dragon Stone," Griffith said. "It is a mystery, even to me."

"Hmph!" snorted the king. "Very well, then. I shall leave my army in your hands."

Army? Drake wondered.

King Roland looked at Drake again.

"Do not let me down, boy," he said. Then he and the soldier left. Everyone sat back down.

The king's words scared Drake. *What will happen if I* do *let him down?* Drake wondered. He had a feeling it wouldn't be good.

Bo took Drake to their room. There was a bed and a wooden chest for each of them. There was also a desk for them to share. A jug of water sat on a table.

"That is your bed," Bo said, pointing.

Drake climbed into bed.

The moon shone through a small window. Drake looked over at Bo. He was already sleeping peacefully. Drake soon drifted off to sleep, too.

All of the sudden, he was in a dark cave.

The air in the cave felt warm. It smelled like the deep, rich dirt where the onions grew. Green eyes glowed in the darkness.

Worm! Worm was in the cave. And behind him were other dragons. They all had the same brown scales and green eyes.

Boom! A loud explosion shook the cave. Smoke filled the air. Worm let out a cry. The dragons slithered across the cave floor, looking for a way out.

Drake woke up in his bed, dripping sweat. *That was some nightmare,* he thought. *It felt so real. . . .*

CHAPTER

8

FLYING PRACTICE

After breakfast the next morning, Drake went back underground with Griffith and the other Dragon Masters.

"Why do we train all the way down here?" Drake asked as they walked.

"Don't you know?" Rori said. "We're a *secret.* No one knows the dragons are here. No one knows the Dragon Stone is real. And no one knows about us."

Drake looked at the wizard.

"It is true," Griffith said. "The king does not want others to know about the dragons."

"Because he's building a dragon army?" Drake asked.

"That is the king's business, not ours," said Griffith. He opened the door to the hallway of dragon caves. "Collect your dragons. We are going outside today."

"Hooray!" yelled Ana, Rori, and Bo.

"But won't someone see us if we go outside?" asked Drake.

"No, we'll be hidden in the Valley of Clouds," said Ana. "Hurry, go get Worm!"

Drake ran through the winding hallway to Worm's cave. Worm raised his head and looked at him. It reminded Drake of his nightmare. He shivered.

"Come on, Worm. We are going outside," Drake said, as he opened the gate.

Worm crawled out of his cave.

Griffith led them all down a dark tunnel.

The tunnel opened up into a bright field of grass. Tall hills rose up on all sides.

"The sun!" cheered Ana. She twirled around.

Drake looked up at the sun and smiled.

"So what do we do out here?" he asked.

Ana grinned. "We fly," she said. She patted Kepri on the head. "Show him, girl."

Kepri raised her long neck and flew straight up. She looped and swirled in the air. Drake watched her, shading his eyes from the sun. He had never seen anything like it.

“Wait till you see Vulcan fly,” Rori said. “Vulcan! Circle!”

Vulcan flapped his big, red wings. He flew up into the sky and circled the field.

“Wow!” Drake said.

He looked over at Bo.

“Your dragon doesn’t have wings, but can she fly, too?” he asked.

Bo nodded. “She does not need wings,” he said. “Shu, please fly.” Shu floated up off the grass.

"It's like she's swimming through the air," Drake said.

"Yes," said Bo. "How Shu flies is very much like how one swims. She can ride the winds."

Drake looked at Worm. His tiny wings did not look like they could lift him. "What about you, Worm?" he asked. "Can you fly, too?"

Worm just stared at Drake. He didn't flap his wings. He didn't even move.

"It's okay," Drake said. He thought of how scared Worm had been in the nightmare. "We can watch the others."

Drake sat on the grass. He put a hand on Worm's back. The dragon moved a little closer to him.

Suddenly, the Dragon Stone felt warm on Drake's skin. He looked down. It was glowing! Drake looked around. Griffith was standing over with the other Dragon Masters. None of their stones were glowing.

Why is my stone glowing? he wondered. *Am I doing something wrong?*

Drake quickly tucked his Dragon Stone inside his shirt. Then he went back to watching the other dragons fly across the sky.

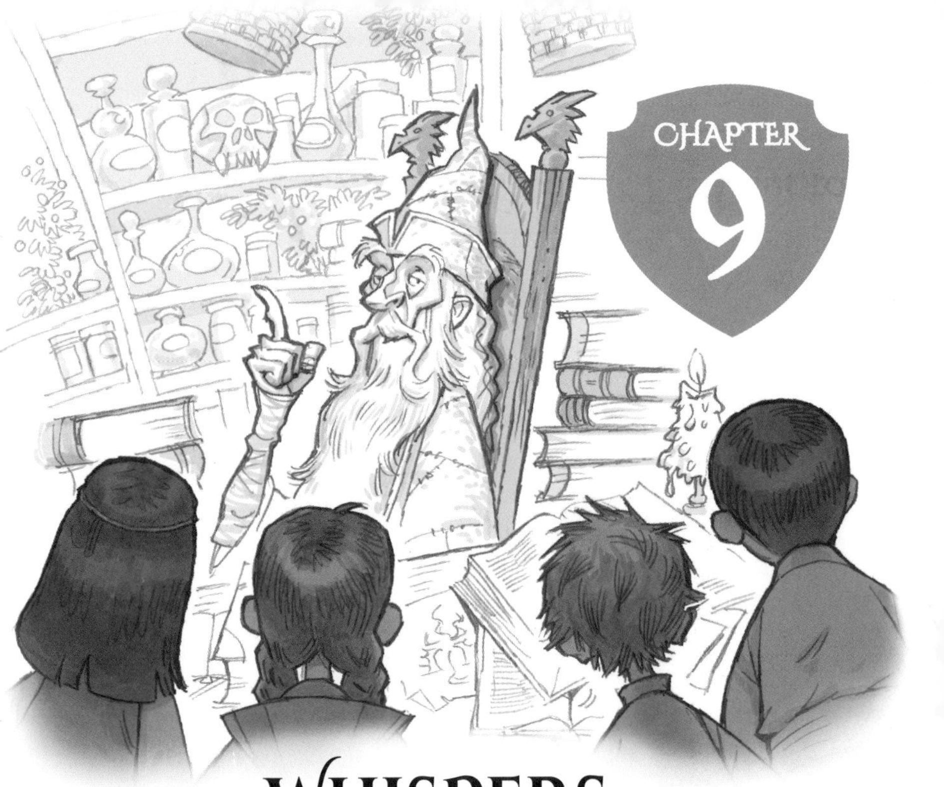

CHAPTER 9

WHISPERS

"And that is how to shine a dragon's scales," Griffith was saying later that week. "Remember, brush one scale at a time. No shortcuts."

Rori sighed. "When can we go out again?"

Drake was glad Rori had asked. They had been stuck in the Training Room for three days.

Drake liked learning about dragons, but he was used to being outside all day every day on his farm back home. He was starting to forget what the sun looked like.

The wizard patted a tall pile of books on his desk. "There is much for you to learn first. We will go out again soon, Rori."

Then a soldier came in. He handed something to Griffith.

The wizard smiled. "Drake, it is a letter for you."

"Read it out loud!" Ana said.

Drake quickly nodded to Griffith.

Dear Drake,

We are glad you are safe. We still don't know why the king brought you there. Can you tell us? Please keep writing so we won't worry. And thank you to your friend Bo for helping you to write to us.

Love,

Your Mother

"Your mother sounds nice," Bo said.

Drake's eyes started to burn. He held back his tears. "Thanks," he said. "May I send another letter to tell her about the dragons?"

"You must not say anything about the dragons," Griffith said. "The king's secret must be kept."

The wizard stood up. "Now, it is time to shine your dragons. Let us go."

As they were leaving the Training Room, Rori ran over to Ana. She started whispering to her.

Drake kept an eye on Rori as they walked toward the dragon caves. *She has a sneaky look on her face*, he thought. *What are she and Ana up to?*

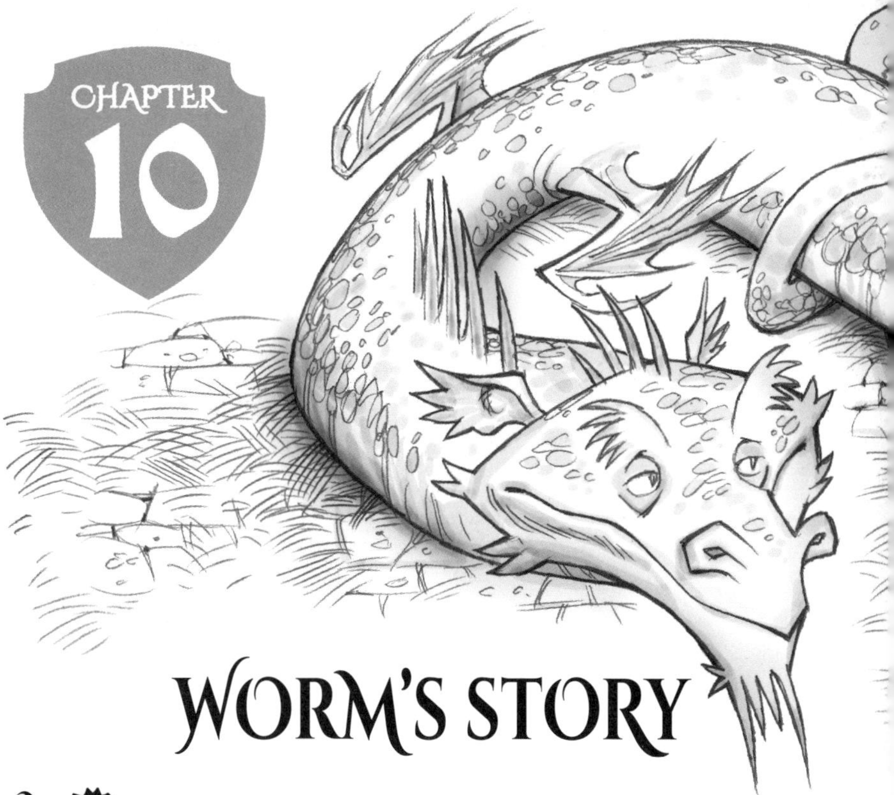

CHAPTER 10

WORM'S STORY

Drake stepped inside Worm's dark cave. Worm opened one eye.

"I need to shine your scales," Drake said. He was carrying a brush, a basket, and towels.

Drake looked at Worm's brown scales. "They're not shiny," he said. "But I'll clean them anyway."

Drake was still getting used to being around Worm. The dragon's head was as big as Drake. Worm could swallow Drake in one gulp if he wanted to. But something about Worm made Drake feel . . . peaceful.

Drake gently brushed one of Worm's scales. The big dragon made a sound low in his throat. Worm smiled and closed his eyes.

“You like that?” Drake asked. Worm made another purring sound. “Good.”

He cleaned Worm’s scales, one at a time.

“I kind of miss the onion field back home,” Drake said to his dragon. “It was hard work. But I loved being outside.”

Drake started to clean Worm’s head.

“And I really miss my family,” Drake said.

He scratched behind Worm's ears, like he did with his cat back home. Then he felt his hand start tingling. . . . He tried to take his hand off Worm, but he couldn't. It was stuck. Drake's eyes widened. He looked at Worm. The dragon was staring hard at him.

Pictures popped into Drake's head. He saw the cave from his nightmare. He saw the explosion again. Before, Drake had woken up. This time, the pictures kept coming. . . .

Worm was trying to get out of the cave, but the other dragons were in the way. Then soldiers rushed into the cave. Each soldier's shirt had a gold dragon sewn on it.

"The king's soldiers?" Drake asked.

The soldiers wrapped Worm in chains. They dragged him out of the cave. *Owwwreeeeee!* Drake could hear Worm's cry. Then his hand stopped tingling. The pictures left his head.

Drake looked at Worm. "Did that really happen? Did the king's men take you away from your family? Just like they took me away from mine?"

Worm nodded.

"I'm so sorry," Drake said. He threw his arms around Worm's neck. Worm closed his eyes.

All his life, Drake had looked up to King Roland. *But why would the king's men treat Worm like a prisoner?* wondered Drake. *Maybe he isn't such a good king after all.*

CHAPTER 11

A NOISE IN THE NIGHT

"Good job cleaning Worm's scales, Drake," Griffith said, walking into the cave.

Drake wasn't going to say anything about what Worm had shown him. Not yet. But he did have a question for Griffith.

"How did the dragons get here?" he asked.

"The king's soldiers searched far and wide," Griffith replied. "It is not easy to find a dragon. Most people have never seen one. But the king did not give up. His soldiers were able to capture these four."

"But did the dragons *want* to come here?" Drake asked.

"The king does not always think about what dragons want," Griffith said darkly. "Now come. It is time for supper."

After they ate, Bo and Drake went to their room. Bo was teaching him how to write the alphabet.

Bo drew a capital *D* and a lowercase *d*.

"See?" Bo said. "The big *D* looks like a dragon with a big belly." He drew a picture on the paper.

"Like Vulcan," Drake said with a laugh. Bo laughed, too.

Moonlight glinted off Bo's Dragon Stone. It reminded Drake of something he'd wanted to ask Bo about.

"Does your stone ever glow?" Drake asked.

Bo shook his head. "No," he said. "Why do you ask?"

"It's just . . . I thought I saw mine glow once," Drake said. "When I was with Worm."

"That's interesting," Bo said. "You should tell Griffith."

Drake nodded. "Tomorrow," he said.

Drake wrote rows of the letter *D* before he went to sleep. He thought he would dream of *D*s – or maybe of Worm again. But just after he climbed into bed . . .

Thunk! Drake heard a loud noise. He sat up and saw two figures standing by Bo's bed!

A SNEAKY PLAN

The two figures turned around. It was Rori and Ana!

"What do *you* want?" Drake asked.

"Go back to sleep," Rori snapped.

"Why should I?" he snapped back. Drake was tired of Rori being so bossy.

"Yeah, why should he?" Bo said. "And why are you two here?"

Ana spoke up. "We are going to bring our dragons outside while the rest of the castle is asleep. Do you guys want to come? You can bring Worm and Shu."

"This is a bad idea," Bo said.

"No, it's not!" Rori said. "We're Dragon Masters! We should be able to take our dragons out whenever we want to."

"You have a point," Drake agreed. "And I do think Worm would like to go outside again."

Bo looked worried. "What if Griffith finds out?" he asked. "What if *the king* finds out?"

"They won't find out," Rori said. "So long as neither of you say anything." She looked them both in the eyes.

"Well, come on, then!" said Ana.

Drake slipped on his shoes. He followed the others down the hall. The door to Griffith's room was open. He was snoring loudly.

ZZZZzzzzzzzzzzzzzz!

Rori put a finger to her lips. *"Shhh!"*

As they tiptoed past the door, Drake peeked inside. The wizard's long beard flew up every time he snored.

The Dragon Masters walked down the stairs. The guard in front of the Training Room door was asleep, too.

"That's Simon," Rori whispered. "He always falls asleep."

They tiptoed past Simon and into the Training Room. The torches were not lit, so the room was black. Rori lit a candle. Then she passed candles to each of them.

"Now, let's get the dragons!" she said, still whispering.

They reached Vulcan's cave first. Rori opened the gate.

"Wake up, Vulcan," she said. "We're going outside."

Grumbling, Vulcan got to his feet. Ana and Bo woke up their dragons. Drake went into Worm's cave.

"Worm, do you want to go outside?" Drake asked.

Worm lifted his head. His eyes shot wide open. They stared right at Drake. Drake got a strange feeling.

"Come on, Worm," Drake said.

But Worm didn't move. He just stared at Drake. *Is he trying to tell me something?* Drake wondered.

Rori, Ana, and Bo walked up to Worm's cave with their dragons.

"Is Worm coming?" Rori asked.

Suddenly, Drake froze. He heard words inside his head: *Do not go into the tunnel!*

CHAPTER 13

TROUBLE IN THE TUNNEL

Did Worm just speak to me . . . through his thoughts? Drake did not know what to think. But he had a feeling those words of warning had come from Worm.

"Drake, what's the matter?" Ana asked.

"It's . . . I'm not sure," he said. *What would they think if I told them I just heard words in my head?* "Worm doesn't want to go."

"Fine. Stay here. Be a big chicken," Rori snapped.

"I didn't say I was staying," Drake shot back. "I'll come along without Worm."

As soon as he said it, Worm crawled out of the cave.

"Look! He is coming with us!" Ana said.

Drake didn't hear any more words in his head. Maybe Worm had changed his mind.

Rori led Vulcan forward. "Let's get moving."

They headed into the long tunnel that led outside. The torches on the walls weren't lit. And their candles weren't doing much to light things up.

"Kepri can light the way," Ana said. But before she could give the command, Rori cried out, "Look!"

Drake craned his neck to look around the dragons in front of him. Then he saw it. A glowing, red orb floated toward them. It grew bigger and bigger as it got closer.

"That looks like wizard's magic!" Ana cried.

"But it is not Griffith's magic," said Bo. "It feels . . . scary."

Just then, Vulcan let out a loud roar. His big tail thrashed back and forth.

"Calm down, Vulcan!" Rori yelled. But her dragon was very upset.

Whack! Whack! Vulcan's tail banged against the sides of the tunnel. His big body slammed against the walls. Kepri and Shu cried out. They both tried to turn back. Only Worm stayed calm.

The tunnel began to shake. Dirt fell from the walls. The Dragon Masters all looked at one another.

"Run!" Drake yelled, but it was too late.

The walls caved in around them!

CHAPTER 14

TRAPPED!

Drake ducked as dirt rained down. He closed his eyes tight.

Then the shaking stopped. Drake opened his eyes.

All the candles had gone out. He looked behind him in the darkness. "Worm, are you all right?"

Worm looked fine. In fact, he didn't have any dust on him. Everybody else was pretty dirty.

"Is everybody okay?" Drake asked.

Ana was on the ground. Bo helped her up.

"I'm fine," she said. "That was scary, though!"

Rori walked over. "I'm sorry," she said. "I don't know why that weird ball of light made Vulcan freak out."

Drake looked around. "Thankfully, it's gone now."

"We should get back," Bo said nervously.

Drake looked past Worm. The tunnel was blocked with rocks and dirt.

"I don't think we can," Drake said.

"The way outside is blocked, too," Rori said.

"We're trapped!" said Bo. He turned pale.

Ana's dragon made a sad sound.

"It's okay, Kepri," Ana said, stroking Kepri's snout. "Can you give us some light, please?"

Kepri opened her mouth and a beautiful, white ball of light came out. The light hung in the air.

"Vulcan is strong," Rori said. "He should be able to push through the rocks."

Vulcan was calmer now that the red orb was gone. He pushed at the rock wall, but the rocks didn't budge.

"Come on, Vulcan!" Rori urged him. But Vulcan couldn't break through.

Bo spoke up. "I could have Shu blast through the rocks with water."

Ana frowned. "What if it doesn't work? Then the tunnel will fill with water."

Everybody was quiet. They knew Ana was right. They were stuck.

Drake looked at Worm. "Sorry I got you into this," he whispered.

Then Worm's green eyes started to glow. A green light swept from the top of Worm's head to the end of his tail.

Drake jumped back. "Worm?" He felt something warm on his chest. He looked down to see that his Dragon Stone was glowing, too!

Ana, Rori, and Bo's mouths dropped open. They stared at Worm and Drake. Worm's green glow filled the tunnel.

"Drake, it looks like your dragon's going to explode!" Rori yelled.

CHAPTER 15

WORM'S SURPRISE

Worm didn't explode. Instead, the dragon closed his eyes.

Then the rocks blocking the tunnel began to shake.

"What's happening?!" Bo yelled.

"Is Worm doing that?" asked Ana.

"I think . . . I think he's using the power of his mind," Drake said. He wasn't sure how he knew. He just did.

Rori, Ana, and Bo stepped back. The rocks kept shaking. Then . . .

Poof! The rocks broke up into tiny pieces. Rock dust filled the air. Drake coughed, waving the dust away with his hand. All of the fallen rocks were gone. The tunnel was clear again!

Drake hugged Worm. "You did it, Worm!"

"We should get out of here before Vulcan sneezes from all this dust," said Rori. "The last time he sneezed he turned my bread into toast."

"Rori's right," said Bo. "Let's get out of here."

Drake stepped through the pile of rubble – and found himself face-to-face with Griffith. Simon the guard stood behind Griffith.

"You are all in *big* trouble!" the wizard said. "The whole castle is awake. And King Roland is furious!"

CHAPTER

16

JUST THE BEGINNING

The group walked back through the tunnel in silence. Six of the king's guards were waiting for them in the Training Room. One stepped forward as soon as they entered the room.

"King Roland wants a report!" he barked.

The Dragon Masters all looked to Griffith.

He cleared his throat. "Please tell King Roland that everything is fine," he said. "The dragons tried to escape. But the Dragon Masters stopped them."

"But —" Drake started to speak, but something about Griffith's look told him to stay quiet.

The soldier nodded to Griffith. "Very well," he said. Then the soldiers and Simon left.

Drake turned to Griffith. "But the dragons didn't do anything wrong," he said.

Rori stepped forward. “Drake’s right. This was my fault. I wanted to take the dragons outside,” she said. She turned to the Dragon Masters. “I’m sorry. It was a bad idea.”

“Agreed,” said Griffith. “Now tell me: How did you all get *out* of the collapsed tunnel?”

“Worm saved us!” Rori cried.

Ana nodded. “He glowed all green. It was amazing!”

“And he turned the rocks to dust!” Bo added.

The wizard's eyes lit up. "That's excellent!" He grabbed Drake by the shoulders. "I knew you could bring it out of him, Drake!"

"Earth Dragons have great power," Griffith said. "Worm has been hiding his power. Until now. He glowed because he was using it."

"Is that why my Dragon Stone glowed, too?" Drake asked.

"No. The stone glows when you have a strong link with your dragon," Griffith said. "The link is strong when you and your dragon can read each other's thoughts. It will happen to the other Dragon Masters, too, in time."

Drake remembered the words he had heard in his head.

"Thank you, Worm," he said, stroking him. "You really saved us today."

"Wait! We forgot to tell you about the red ball of light," Rori piped up. "That's what scared Vulcan. When it flew into the tunnel, he panicked and made the tunnel collapse."

A cloud came over Griffith's face. "Are you sure that you saw a *red* ball of light?"

All four Dragon Masters nodded.

"This is serious," Griffith said. "Danger may be heading our way."

"Danger?" Bo asked.

Griffith patted Bo's head. "For now, we are safe. Let's all get some sleep."

As Drake led Worm back to his cave, he felt a strong connection to his dragon. He wasn't going back to the onion fields. This was his life now — a life full of dragons and magic and danger.

He was a Dragon Master.

TRACEY WEST spends a lot of time thinking about what kind of dragon would be best for her to make friends with. Like Drake, she likes to dig in the garden (but she always wears gloves in case of worms!), so an Earth Dragon might be the answer.

Tracey has written dozens of books for kids. She does her writing in the house she shares with her husband and three stepkids. She also has plenty of animal friends to keep her company. She has two dogs, seven chickens, and one cat, who sits on her desk when she writes! Thankfully, the cat does not weigh as much as a dragon.

GRAHAM HOWELLS lives with his wife and two sons in west Wales, a place full of castles, and legends of wizards and dragons.

There are many stories about the dragons of Wales. One story tells of a large, legless dragon—sort of like Worm! Graham's home is also near where Merlin the great wizard is said to lie asleep in a crystal cave.

Graham has illustrated several books. He has created artwork for film, television, and board games, too. Graham also writes stories for children. In 2009, he won the Tir Na N'Og award for *Merlin's Magical Creatures*.

Questions and Activities

Look at the picture on top of page 10. How do you think Rori **FEELS** about Drake?

Why does Worm follow Drake through the tunnel even though he warned Drake not to go?

How does Worm **SAVE** the Dragon Masters?

Why do you think the Dragon Masters confess to Griffith that it was their idea to bring the dragons outside?

If you had a dragon, what kind of special power would you want it to have? **DRAW** a picture of your dragon performing the special power.

scholastic.com/branches